Sleep Tight, Little One

SLEEP TIGHT, LITTLE ONE
A Collection of Stories for Bedtime

LITTLE TIGER PRESS
An imprint of Magi Publications
1 The Coda Centre, 189 Munster Road,
London SW6 6AW
www.littletigerpress.com

First published in Great Britain 2008
This volume copyright © Magi Publications 2008
Cover illustration copyright © Alison Edgson 2008

LITTLE BEAR'S SPECIAL WISH
Gillian Lobel
Illustrated by Gaby Hansen
First published in Great Britain 2003
by Little Tiger Press
An imprint of Magi Publications
Text copyright © Gillian Lobel 2003
Illustrations copyright © Gaby Hansen 2003

NEWTON
Rory Tyger
First published in Great Britain 2001
by Little Tiger Press
An imprint of Magi Publications
Text and Illustrations copyright
© Rory Tyger 2001

HAVE YOU GOT MY PURR?
Judy West
Illustrated by Tim Warnes
First published in Great Britain 1999
by Little Tiger Press
An imprint of Magi Publications
Text copyright © Judy West 1999
Illustrations copyright © Tim Warnes 1999

GOODNIGHT, LITTLE HARE
Sheridan Cain
Illustrated by Sally Percy
First published in Great Britain 1999
by Little Tiger Press
An imprint of Magi Publications
Text copyright © Sheridan Cain 1999
Illustrations copyright © Sally Percy 1999

Sleep Tight, Little One

A Collection of Stories for Bedtime

LITTLE TIGER PRESS
London

Contents

LITTLE BEAR'S SPECIAL WISH
Gillian Lobel & Gaby Hansen

9

NEWTON
Rory Tyger

37

HAVE YOU GOT MY PURR?

Judy West & Tim Warnes

65

GOODNIGHT, LITTLE HARE

Sheridan Cain & Sally Percy

93

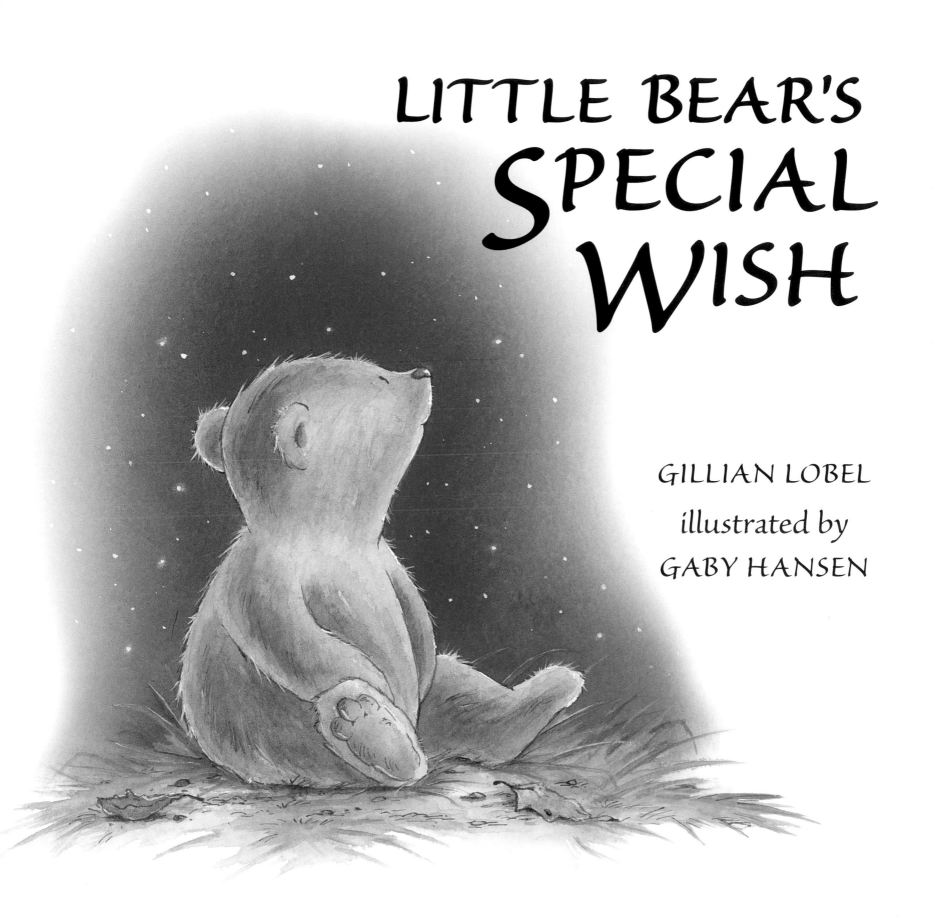

LITTLE BEAR'S
SPECIAL
WISH

GILLIAN LOBEL

illustrated by

GABY HANSEN

The sun was still in bed when
Little Brown Bear crept out into the shadowy woods.
"I wish, I wish . . ." he whispered.
"You're up early, Little Brown Bear!" called Lippity
Rabbit. "What are you wishing for?"
"It's my mummy's birthday," said Little Brown Bear,
"and I wish I could find the most special present
in all the world for her."
"I'll help you!" said Lippity Rabbit.
So off they went along the winding path. Little pools
of moonlight danced around their feet.

In the middle of the woods was a big rock.

Little Brown Bear sat down for a moment to think.

High above him glittered a star, so big and

bright he could almost touch it.

"I know – I could give my mummy a star,"

he said. "That would be a very special present."

Little Brown Bear gave
a little jump. But he
could not reach the star.

He gave a very big jump.
But still he could not reach
the star. Then Little Brown
Bear had an idea.

"I know!" he said. "If we climb to the very top of the hill, then we will be able to reach the stars!"

From the top of the hill the stars looked even brighter – and much nearer, too. Little Brown Bear stretched up on to his tiptoes. But the stars were still too far away. Then Little Brown Bear had a very good idea indeed.

"I know!" he said. "We must build
a big, big tower to the stars!"
"I'll help you!" said
Lippity Rabbit.

Together they piled the biggest stones they could find,
one on top of the other. Then they stepped back and looked.
A stone stairway stretched to the stars. "Now I shall reach
a star for my mummy," said Little Brown Bear happily.
He climbed right to the top and stretched out a paw.
But still he couldn't reach the stars.

"I know!" called Lippity Rabbit. "If I climb on your shoulders, then I can knock a star down with my long, loppy ears!"

Lippity Rabbit scrambled on to Little Brown Bear's shoulders. He stretched up his long, loppy ears. He waggled them furiously.

"Be careful, Lippity!" called Little Brown Bear. "You're making me wobble!"

Suddenly Little Brown Bear felt
something tapping his foot.
   "Can I help you?" croaked a voice.
   "Why yes, Very Small Frog,"
    said Little Brown Bear. "Are you
    any good at jumping?"
   Very Small Frog puffed out his chest.
   "Just watch me!" he said.
 High into the air he flew, and landed
 right between Lippity Rabbit's long,
    loppy ears.

 "Can you reach the brightest star from there?"
   asked Little Brown Bear.
 "No problem!" shouted Very Small Frog.
   He took a mighty breath. "Look out, stars,
   here I come!" he shouted.

Very Small Frog gave a great push with his strong back legs. Up, up, up he sailed. Lippity Rabbit's long, loppy ears twirled round and round. "Help!" he shouted. "Somebody save me!"

Backwards and forwards he swayed, and backwards and forwards swayed Little Brown Bear. With a mighty crash the stone tower toppled to the ground. And down and down tumbled Lippity Rabbit and Little Brown Bear.

"I can't breathe, Lippity!" gasped Little
Brown Bear. "You're sitting right on by dose!"

Then Very Small Frog sailed down from the
stars and landed on Lippity Rabbit's head.
"I'm sorry, Little Brown Bear," he said. "I
jumped right over the moon, but I still
couldn't reach the stars."

Little Brown Bear sat up carefully.

His nose was scratched and his head hurt.

"Now my special wish will *never* come true,"
he said. "I shall never find a star for my mummy!"

"Don't be sad, Little Brown Bear," said Lippity Rabbit.

And he gave him a big hug.

A tear ran down Little Brown Bear's nose, and
splashed into a tiny pool at his feet.

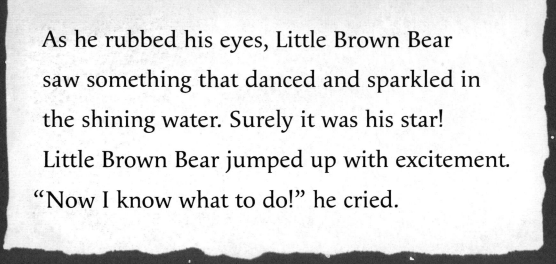

As he rubbed his eyes, Little Brown Bear
saw something that danced and sparkled in
the shining water. Surely it was his star!
Little Brown Bear jumped up with excitement.
"Now I know what to do!" he cried.

Off he ran down the hillside.

"Wait for us!" cried Lippity Rabbit
and Very Small Frog.

Through the ferny woods they ran, over the silver meadows, until they reached the stream. For a long time they hunted along the sandy shore until Little Brown Bear found just what he was looking for. Then carefully, carefully, he carried it all the way home.

"Happy birthday, Mummy!" he cried.

Into his mother's lap he placed a pearly shell that
shone like a rainbow. There, in the heart of the shell,
a tiny pool of water quivered. And in that pool a
very special star shimmered and shook – the star
that had made a little bear's birthday wish come true.

"Lippity Rabbit and Very Small Frog helped me find
the shell, but I caught the star all by myself!" said
Little Brown Bear proudly.

Mother Bear knelt down and gave him a big hug.

"Thank you all very much," she said. "This is
a very special birthday present indeed!"

newton

by
Rory Tyger

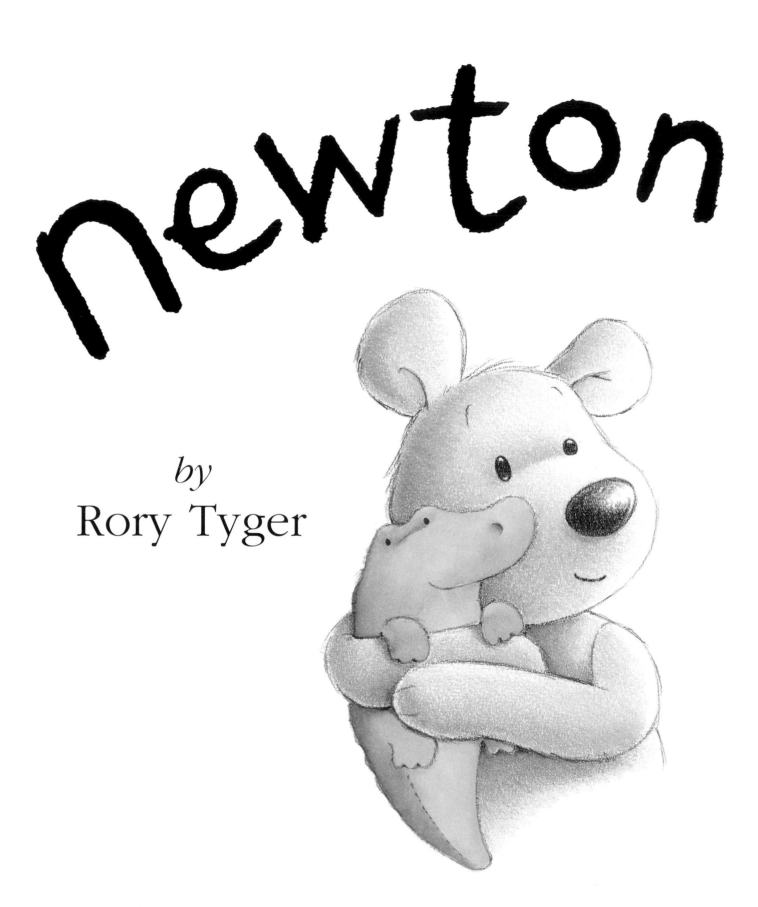

CREAK, CREAK, CRE-E-EAK

Newton woke up suddenly.
There was a funny noise somewhere in the
room. "Don't be frightened," he told Woffle.
"There's always an explanation for everything."
He gave each of his toys a special cuddle
so they wouldn't be scared.

CREAK, CREAK, CRE-E-EAK

went the noise again.

Newton got out of bed and turned on the light.
He walked across the room . . .

"See, toys," he said. "There's nothing to be frightened of. It's only the wardrobe door!"

Newton went back to bed again.

FLAP! FLAP! FLAP!

What was that? Was it a ghost?

Once more Newton got out of bed. He wasn't really scared, but he took his bravest toy, Snappy, just in case. He tiptoed, very quietly, towards the noise.

FLAP! FLAP! FLAP!

it went again. "Of course!" said Newton . . .

"Just what I thought."
It was his bedroom curtains,
flapping in the breeze.
"I'll soon sort those out,"
said Newton.

"You were very brave,
Snappy," he said, as
he closed the window.

SPLISH!
SPLASH!
SPLISH!

Another noise!

Newton looked outside. It wasn't raining.
Besides, the noise wasn't coming from
outside.

Nor was it coming from
his bedroom. What was it?
"Stay right there, you two,"
said Newton, "while I look
around."

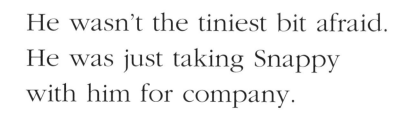

He wasn't the tiniest bit afraid.
He was just taking Snappy
with him for company.

Newton crept down the corridor. It was
very spooky, especially in the dark corners.

SPLISH! SPLASH! SPLISH!

went the noise.

Very, very quietly, Newton
opened the bathroom door . . .

"Of course, we knew it was the bathroom
tap, didn't we, Snappy," said Newton.

Newton turned off the tap, and tiptoed back down the corridor. "Shh," he said to Snappy, just in case *something* in the dark corners sprang out at them.

Before he got into bed, Newton pulled back the curtains – just to check. It was very, very quiet outside. "No more funny noises," said Newton.

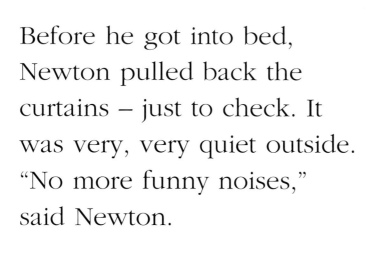

"You can go to sleep now," he told all his toys.

RUMBLE! RUMBLE! RUMBLE!

"Oh no!" cried Newton. "What's that?"

Newton listened very hard. Not a sound. He was just beginning to think he hadn't heard anything at all when

RUMBLE! RUMBLE! RUMBLE!

There it was again!

Newton peered under his bed.
Nothing there at all – except for
an old sweet he'd forgotten about.
"Don't worry," said Newton. "We'll
soon find out what it is."

RUMBLE!
Newton stood
very still.

RUMBLE!
Newton listened
very hard.

RUMBLE! went the noise.
And suddenly Newton knew
exactly what it was!

Newton padded downstairs, and into the kitchen. He helped himself to a large glass of milk and two thick slices of bread and honey. And now he could hear no

RUMBLE! RUMBLE! RUMBLE!

at all, because . . .

the rumbling had been
his empty tummy!

Newton went upstairs again, and told his toys
about his rumbling tummy.
"There's always an explanation for everything,"
said Newton, as he climbed back into bed.
"Goodnight, everyone . . ."

"Sleep tight!"

SNORE, SNORE, SNORE,

went Newton.

60

Have you got my Purr?

by
Judy West and Tim Warnes

"Oh Mummy, Mummy!"

"What's the matter, little Kitten?
Why are you crying?"

"Oh Mummy, Mummy, I've lost my purr."

"You'll find your purr, little Kitten.
Just wait and see."

66

"Oh Dog, Dog, have you got my purr?"

"Woof, woof," said Dog, licking his bone.

"I haven't got your purr, little Kitten.

This is my *woof*. Why don't you ask Cow?"

"Oh Cow, Cow, have
you got my purr?"
"Moo, moo," said Cow,
flicking flies with
her ears.

70

"I haven't got your purr,
little Kitten. This is my *moo*.
Why don't you ask Pig?"

71

"Oh Pig, Pig, have you got my purr?"
"Oink, oink," said Pig, snuffling
in the straw.

"I haven't got your purr, little Kitten. This is my *oink*. Why don't you ask Duck?"

73

"Oh Duck, Duck, have you got my purr?"
"Quack, quack," said Duck, splashing in the water.

"I haven't got your purr, little Kitten. This is my *quack*. Why don't you ask Mouse?"

"Oh Mouse, Mouse, have you got my purr?"
"Squeak, squeak," said Mouse, nibbling cheese
in the barn. "I haven't got your purr, little Kitten.
This is my *squeak*. Why don't you ask Sheep?"

SQUEAK SQUEAK

"Oh Sheep, Sheep, have you got my purr?"
"Baa, baa," said Sheep, munching grass in
the field. "I haven't got your purr, little Kitten.
This is my *baa*. Why don't you ask wise old Owl?"

"Wise old Owl, have you got my purr?"
"Hoot, hoot," said the wise old Owl, blinking his big round eyes.

"I haven't got your purr, little Kitten. This is my *hoot*. Why don't you go back and ask your mother?"

"Oh Mummy, Mummy," wailed little Kitten. "*Nobody's* got my purr.

Dog hasn't got it. He's got a woof.

Cow hasn't got it. She's got a moo.

Pig hasn't got it. She's got an oink.

Duck hasn't got it. She's got a quack.

Mouse hasn't got it. He's got a squeak.

Sheep hasn't got it. She's got a baa.

Wise old Owl hasn't got it. He's got a hoot.

Oh Mummy, Mummy, I've lost my purr!"

84

"You haven't lost your purr,
little Kitten. Come here
and I'll explain."

"Nobody's got your purr.
Your purr is inside you
when you're happy!
Listen, little Kitten,
listen . . ."

"My *purr!*
Oh, Mummy.
I've found my purr!
It was here
all the time."
So little Kitten
curled up . . .

and purred and purred
and purred.

GOODNIGHT, LITTLE HARE

Sheridan Cain

illustrated by
Sally Percy

By the pale light of the moon Mother Hare
sat watching Little Hare. He lay with eyes tight
shut. For his blanket he had the sky, and the
soft hay formed his bed.

"Goodnight, Little Hare," she whispered.

Mole trundled by, and almost toppled over Little Hare.
"Mother Hare," he said, "you cannot leave your baby there.
It isn't safe, for the farmer cuts the hay at dawn."

"But what can I do?" asked Mother Hare. "Where can
Little Hare sleep?"

"You should dig a hole, big and deep," said Mole.
"That's where your little baby should sleep."

So Mother Hare began to dig.

She scraped and scraped
at the soft brown earth, until
the hole was big and deep. Then
she carried Little Hare to his new bed.

But Little Hare did not
like it. "Mama," he cried.
"It's so dark and I'm afraid."

Badger came bumbling along and heard
Little Hare's cry. "Mother Hare," he said,
"you cannot leave your baby there. It isn't safe.
Weasel's hunting through hole and burrow,
and he will soon find Little Hare."

"But what can I do?" asked Mother Hare. "Where can Little Hare sleep?" "You should cover him in a bed of leaves. That will fool Weasel," said Badger.

So Mother Hare hurried
and she scurried.

She formed the leaves
into a soft round pile.
Then she carried Little
Hare to his new bed.

But Little Hare did not like it.
"Mama," he cried. "I'm so afraid. I don't like
the crinkly crackly noise my new bed makes."

Blackbird was up early, pecking among the
leaves for grubs when he heard Little Hare's cry.

"Mother Hare," he said, "you cannot leave your
baby there. It isn't safe. Fox's nose is sharp,
and he will soon sniff out Little Hare."

"But what can I do?" asked Mother Hare.

"Where can Little Hare sleep?"

"What you need is a nest
up high," said Blackbird.

"Fox will never reach
him there."

So Mother Hare leapt up
on to the branch of a tree,
and placed Little Hare
in an empty bird's nest.

But Little Hare did not like it.
"Mama," he cried, looking down.
"I'm so afraid. It's high up here
and I might fall out."

Mother Hare carried Little Hare down again. She did not know what to do. "Oh dear," she sobbed. "How can I find a bed that's safe for Little Hare?"

Owl was watching
Mother Hare and Little
Hare from his perch.

"Don't be sad," said Owl.
"Don't you remember when *you*
were young, and how *your* mother
kept you safe?"

Mother Hare remembered the sky
that was her blanket. She remembered
the soft golden hay that was her bed.

She remembered how, from
dusk to dawn, her mother
had watched over her.

The sun was just rising.
Mother Hare looked
towards the field that
was her home, and her
eyes became bright. The
farmer had come early,
and the hay was cut.
It was quite safe
there now.

Mother Hare carried
Little Hare back to his
old bed and laid him
gently down.

116

"Mama," said Little Hare.
"I'm not afraid now. This
is my own bed, and I like it."

Goodnight, Little Hare!